The
KNIGHT'S CHAIN

A Chained Gods Series Story, Vol 1.5

Tamira Thayne

This book is a work of fiction. Names, characters, places, and incidents are either
the product of the author's imagination or are used fictitiously, and any resemblance
to actual persons, living or dead, business establishments, events, government
agencies, or locales is entirely coincidental or fictitious.

Published by Who Chains You Publishing
P.O. Box 581
Amissville, VA 20106
www.WhoChainsYou.com

Story, Design, and layout by Tamira Thayne
www.TamiraThayne.com

ISBN-13: 978-1-946044-31-0

Printed in the United States of America

First Edition

In Memory of our beloved Rosie Bear,
who was found dragging a chain along
a country road; she taught me
the awesomeness of all things Akita.

You were a Queen to me, girl.

Also by Tamira Thayne

AUTHOR OF
The King's Tether:
A Chained Gods Series Prequel Story

The Wrath of Dog:
The Chained Gods Series Book 1

The Curse of Cur:
The Chained Gods Series Book 2

Foster Doggie Insanity:
Tips and Tales to Keep your Kool as a Doggie Foster Parent

Capitol in Chains: 54 Days of the Doghouse Blues

Smidgey Pidgey's Predicament

Raffy Calfy's Rescue

Happy Dog Coloring Book: From Chained to Cherished

EDITOR OF
Rescue Smiles: Favorite Animal Stories
of Love and Liberation

More Rescue Smiles: Beloved Animal Tales
of Freedom and Devotion

Unchain My Heart: Dogs Deserve Better Rescue
Stories of Courage, Compassion, and Caring

Contents

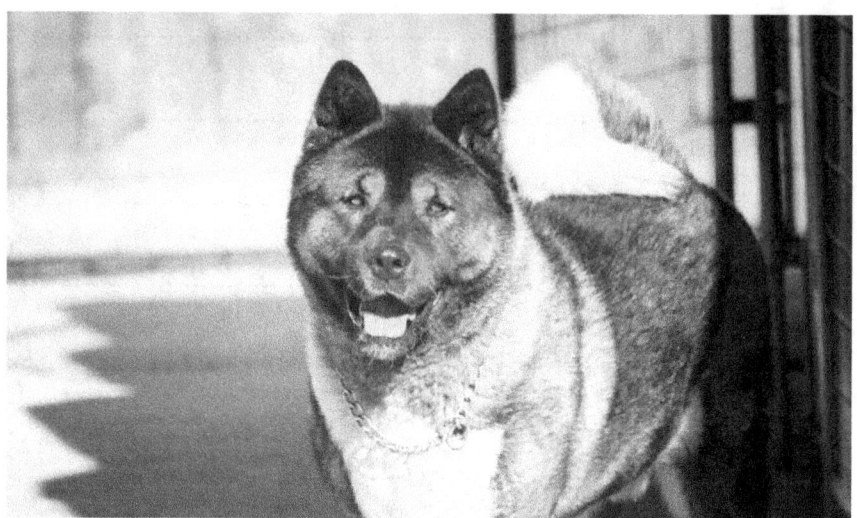

Sprinkles (yes, he is a male) is a gorgeous Akita, and the inspiration for Curjan's dog form. Photo courtesy of JoAnn Dimon, Big East Akita Rescue. B.E.A.R. is a 501(c)3 nonprofit, hands-on, Akita rescue group covering the NY, NJ, and PA metropolitan regions and the Northeast. The group rescues unwanted, abused, and neglected Akitas in need. This gorgeous boy was rescued from the Portage Ohio Animal Shelter. Learn more or donate at bigeastakitarescue.org.

Author Disclaimer: This is a work of fiction. My character, Curjan, is trying to survive an abusive imprisonment. In order to do so, he must fight back against men who abducted and tortured him, and is by no means "an aggressive dog". I chose an Akita for my knight because I love their looks and personalities, finding them both regal and commanding. I've fostered and loved many an Akita, and the breed will always hold a portion of my heart. If there is any message that I'm putting front and center throughout this book series, it would be that chaining increases the odds of aggression in ALL canines—a fact acknowledged by the CDC in noting that chaining as a primary means of confinement ups the likelihood of aggression in dogs almost threefold.

KILLING MACHINE

❖

The Akita was massive, a fine example of the breed—with the single exception of his current physical state: skeletal, matted, and attached to a cement post by a thick logging chain. He refused to let those things bother him, however; they were mere nuisances, after all.

What mattered most to him was that he was a killing machine, and any men in black who crossed his path would die.

Simple as that.

He was done with the torture, had enough of the domination; who were these men to treat him as a mongrel, a cur? Where was the respect he instinctively knew he'd earned and demanded in better days?

His mind may have been jumbled, with memories of the past escaping him—but he knew one thing for sure: he was more than this beast on a chain.

Knew he was born for greater things, knew he mattered somewhere; if only he could get back to wherever, whatever, whenever that was.

For now, he would wait...and, if possible, slay each and every one of his abductors who came within snapping distance of his massive jaws.

Destroying the men in black had become the primary focus of his bitter existence. Any monster who starved a living being, who chained a magnificent canine and deprived him or her of water and shelter? Must die.

For him, this much was black and white.

He held firm to a code of ethics. He knew what was happening to him and the retriever chained nearby was depraved, and therefore—to his mind—anyone taking part in it was evil and he felt no compunction about ending them.

He bolted to the perimeter of his chain length, stopping short as he hit the outermost edge—just before he would have felt the sharp, backward yank.

The circumference of the time-worn path left him a mere 20 feet of exercise space. He paced and leapt as much as he could throughout the day, despite the overwhelming hunger and thirst that attacked his physical and mental well-being. He was determined to keep his body and his wits as sharp as possible, eager for the moment he could engineer an escape.

Each day when he woke he renewed his vow to free himself, free the retriever too.

Gut instinct told him that he'd been on a mission that was thwarted by this confinement, that he was meant to be doing something else, somewhere else. The mental fog that kept him from remembering angered, confused, and frustrated him.

He was also aware that there was something off about this chain—he was being controlled through it, and it needed to stop.

But the thick iron links of the chain, now well-rusted,

were too unyielding.

In the beginning, when he still had strength and momentum on his side, he would spend all day pulling on the chain, gnawing its most vulnerable parts, and he'd gotten nowhere.

It was too strong; not only that, but it emitted vibrations that were not consistent with those a normal chain should be putting off.

He needed free of it.

Today would not be that day.

He slumped down, head on his paws, and drifted into an uneasy sleep.

Another Dimension

He was immortal. The knowledge flashed into his dream like it did every night, along with his name. *Curjan.* It was Curjan.

He tried to implant the seed, the seed of his birth name into his memory, so he could unearth it upon awakening. He feared he would once more fail to hold onto it as he'd done so many times in the past.

Curjan. A name! He was more than just a dog—albeit a magnificent one, his admiration of the breed rushing to the fore. In the dream state, he eyed his pelt and his Akita frame the way he used to look—toned, well-muscled, bathed, and groomed.

But not only that…he could shift into and out of the form of a man!

He was a knight in the king's army, one of his personal guard, to be exact. Curjan took his job extremely seriously, allowing no one to sway him from his objectives, which were protecting the king and carrying out his orders. He took pride in his team of eight elite guardsmen and women.

He briefly recalled their final mission: they had traveled to Earth to find a woman, a mate for the king, and spent many months seeking her before achieving success. That triumph was hard-won, and he'd never witnessed the king so happy, so fulfilled.

But what had gone wrong? How did he go from that fortunate happenstance to this moment, so many years later—chained in Akita form, starving, thirsty, enraged, and murderous?

He needed answers, and time and again found only blanks.

He traveled further into his past while he could, seeking his earliest childhood memories. He remembered two parents who loved him, remembered being held in their arms, nurtured, cherished, respected. Then disaster struck, and all semblance of security was ripped from him in one of the worst natural catastrophes ever experienced on his dimension.

Turns out there are things even the immortals of Perrin couldn't bounce back from—being blown apart by an underground volcanic eruption was one of them.

His life had changed forever after the loss of his parents.

He'd been just ten years old, a mere baby in his world. Luckily, on Perrin orphans were valued, not tossed aside to live amongst the riffraff the way they often were on Earth. He went into the king's palace and stayed there with the other foster children. There they were showered with attention and loving kindness by women who couldn't bear children or who had suffered grievous losses of their own.

When they reached the age of thirteen, if they so desired and had an aptitude for it, they were given combat training. The training made it possible for them to work in the guard and other forces needed to keep the peace and protect the Perrin dimension when they came of age.

Even though Curjan grieved his parents deeply every day, he could not have said he wanted for anything—with the exception of that deep soul connection one often feels to one's own biological family.

Determined to succeed despite his losses, Curjan spent most of his days in training, his sole goal being to impress the king, become part of his select team.

His first chance came at the age of fifteen, when he was drilling with squad members high up on the Perrasian mountain slopes. He'd overtaken the leader on the race to the highest peak, grabbed the flag, and hurried down again, desperately wanting to be first, to win the round.

Along the way he'd stopped to provide aid to one of his teammates who'd fallen and injured his leg. While he was helping the boy, another trainee, Joshua, had plucked the flag from his belt and raced ahead of him to home base.

He'd lost.

He hung his head, ashamed to have blown his chance to impress King Randulf, who stood quietly observing the candidates from the sidelines. He kicked at the dirt in frustration, and began to pick his solitary way back to the barracks to drown his sorrows in a long shower.

He was unaware that his teammate had been asked to take a fall so close to the finish line—explicitly as a test for the front runners—to see who chose team over victory. The king sent for him, not Joshua, congratulated him, and let Curjan and the rest of the candidates know he was the true winner of the contest.

King Randulf made it clear to all assembled that winning

was not about who got there first; it was about making it together, being part of a unique force that had each other's backs.

It was a lesson he'd always remember. His loyalty to King Randulf had been cemented from that day forward.

Nearby

S he languished 25 feet from him, a golden retriever, chained and in all respects mired in the same predicament as he was. Her fur went beyond matted, even falling out in places due to lack of nutrition. She was skeletal, sickly, depressed.

When they both paced to the end of their tethers, they reached within four feet of each other, but could never touch.

The two dogs shared some primitive mindlink and could send images to one another, communicating in a limited fashion. They slept as close to one another as possible, both for protection and for the tenuous company of their small pack.

She was more accepting of their shared fate, in truth just wanting to give up and die, but he would not, could not, allow himself that luxury. Both dogs were provided with filthy water and scraps of food once a week—enough to keep them alive, but never enough to thrive.

Their captors ensured it stayed that way.

Whoever was behind their imprisonment wanted the dogs angry and aggressive, and regularly sent men in black to ensure Curjan was still willing to maim, even kill. He never disappointed, and would readily rip out the throat of any man or woman who dared enter his territory.

They'd learned—if they wanted to survive—to come in twos or threes; sending just one often meant he or she did not return.

The golden retriever whined and moaned in her sleep. She sometimes shared images from her dreams with him, the few she could access, which was still a great deal more than he remembered. She too saw her own immortality, a human form, and a home and family that awaited her on another dimension.

Instead of giving her something to fight for, the dreams only made her more depressed and despondent, thus leaving the sole protection of their territory to his discretion. Mostly she lay in the sun or shade and escaped into sleep, alternately moaning, whining, or crying out.

She was pitiful, in truth. And, although he understood the despair and fought the same urges within himself, he knew that if he gave up they would never be free. And THAT he could not accept—for either of them.

So he paced and planned to the extent that his mind fog would allow, working his way through barebones solutions, hoping someday one of them would pay off.

He flashed the retriever a hint of a plan he'd been working on: an image of them luring a single man in black into the space between them. Then they would wrap their chains around both his neck and feet, hold him captive, and threaten his life unless he freed both dogs.

It was a good plan, in theory. The best they had, anyway.

But would it work in practice?

Only time would tell.

A Name Forgotten

His name was within grabbing distance as he dredged his way up from the depths of sleep, but it slipped away again when he opened his eyes, exacerbating the endless cycle of frustration.

Not that it mattered, he guessed. Reality told him that he was a skeletal dog on a chain, leading a miserable existence and unable to die from something as minor as thirst and hunger. What good would a name do him anyway?

If the goal of this confinement had been to break him, it had succeeded, many times over. But it had also built a stronger version of the fighter he knew himself to be, because in the end he couldn't bear to give up, couldn't lay down and die without resistance.

Oh, he'd tried. But his lack of success—and the retriever's, too—gave him an understanding that death was close to an impossibility for him.

For about a year depression had taken hold and he'd waited for death, begged for it. The grim reaper should have met them halfway, given that food and water were so scarce. Mostly they drank from puddles, so if it didn't rain, they didn't drink. And even when it did rain, the water was more often than not poisoned with runoff from the massive heaps of rusting junk surrounding them.

They drank it anyway.

He had no inkling where they were, but the weather was all over the board, with rain, snow, extreme heat, and biting cold, depending on time of the year. They were enclosed on four sides by walls of compressed vehicles, forming an effective prison in addition to the tethers holding them in place. He could sometimes hear the whine of heavy equipment operating nearby, but their position remained relatively quiet and unchanging.

He tried to stay awake as much as he could, to act as sentinel for them, but sleep claimed him more often than not, given his sad state of physical health.

Today when he dreamed, it was different for the first time in forever. Today he dreamed not of his past, but of a tentative future. He saw a girl, a willowy, strong, and determined girl, and felt an instant and—on his part at least—unwanted kinship with her. He felt a rush of need to protect her, to fight by her side, to make sure she stayed alive to gain the happiness she deserved.

When he awoke, he reserved enough of the dream to fill him with a renewed determination to escape. He recalled a shadowy figure of a girl, and his gut told him he needed to get to her.

He knew now they had no choice but to attempt their plan. He only hoped it would work.

BREAKOUT

He forced a few images of the scenario into the retriever's head. She nodded, perking up a little at the prospect of change, of hope.

They didn't have long to wait. It'd been a week since they were allowed food or water, but they'd been lucky in that it had snowed, and they'd eaten the cold clumps and drank the melted water when the temperatures rose.

In a matter of hours, two men in black wound their way through the wreckage to the dogs' area. The Akita knew he had to take one of the men out immediately in order to get the other alone. The retriever would keep the second man busy in the meantime.

The men drifted into the enclosure, laughing and flinging scraps about like they were tossing candy from a Halloween float. The dogs ignored the fare, which wasn't easy given their level of starvation, but they had other plans.

They knew the rations were a means of distracting them so the men could dump fetid liquid into their bowls and hightail it out of there. But not today. At the Akita's signal, both dogs feinted like they were going for the food, but instead lunged at the men as they moved toward the water dishes.

He was first to reach his target, and fastest. She was meant only to hold hers in place while his was slain. He did not disappoint. Grabbing the man by the ankle, he jerked him backward, releasing and then clamping his massive jaws onto the man's waist. As his abductor screamed, kicked, and pushed at him, he clung tenaciously, waiting for his chance to go for the throat.

It was over quickly. As the man thrashed, the Akita lodged his paw onto his chest, holding him in place, and then quickly released and grasped him by his throat, giving a massive rip and ending it. The man bled out all over his territory.

If this plan didn't work, he would lap up the liquid nourishment later, he mused as the blood pooled into a crevice.

Meanwhile, the retriever gripped the other by the leg as he shouted and lashed out at her. She was unshakable, though, the possibility of escape egging her on. She dragged him to the middle area between their tethers, and the Akita raced over, biting his arm and pulling him to the ground and into position. He cocked his neck and spun it counterclockwise to loop the chain about the man's throat.

The retriever did the same at his feet, effectively cocooning him and keeping him from slipping away. The man flailed about, but soon came to understand that he was well and truly caught when the Akita's massive paws pinned his arms to the ground.

It was then that he tried to bargain with them, using a high-pitched "baby talk" tone in an attempt to befriend them.

The Akita barked a laugh, given that this same man had treated them like dirt all these years. Please. He knew his scent. Now he expected them to believe that he actually liked dogs and cared about their welfare?

Their bid for freedom was soon aided by a twist of fate they hadn't seen coming. The three of them—the two dogs and the man in black—became mindlinked together, the chains that were wrapped around the man's neck and ankles serving as a physical conduit between them.

This was the confirmation the Akita sought that these were no ordinary chains...they'd been manipulated by his captors.

Instead of their newfound bond with the man acting to clear the dogs' minds, the man's thinking became more foggy, allowing the dogs to readily influence his actions. Due to this unexpected bounty, the dogs were able to easily place a demand into his mind to release them both from their chains.

Their combined mental strength overtook the man's ability to think rationally, and he in effect became a submissive member of their pack. Instead of the expected resistance to releasing them, they encountered instead compliance, verging on the point of ready acquiescence.

The man sent an image to the pack mind, illustrating that he needed his hands free in order to liberate them. The Akita responded with a vision of one arm being released, not both, and he removed his feet from the man's arms while lifting and imprisoning the left wrist in his powerful jaws. He had a better chance of retaining control of the man if this turned out to be a ploy than the retriever did, and both dogs knew it.

The retriever stood at attention, holding her ground, her chain stretched to its limit with the man trussed up between them.

The dogs held fast to their mindlink, endeavoring to keep the man under their control as they sensed the beginnings of his mental struggle against them. The Akita again insistently forced the instruction into the man's head to release them, and he nodded, but then hesitated again. This time the retriever joined in, emphasizing that this would happen, or death for the man would be the result.

He understood.

With his free hand, he reached to the back of the Akita's neck, placing his thumb over a sensor which allowed him to remove the tether after confirmation of his print. A loud beep ensued, and the chain fell unceremoniously away.

He was FREE! He refused to engage in more than a momentary mental celebration, however, as he still had a job to do: free the retriever, get her to safety, find the girl. Then he could celebrate.

He gave himself the luxury of a minute head shake, relishing the rush of liberation that came with the release of the chain. How long had it been?

He didn't know.

Pushing thoughts of independence aside, he dropped the man's arm and lunged for the chain, which has slacked from about the man's throat upon his release. Luckily, he was faster than his captive, who'd begun to sense an opening for his own freedom and make a bid for it.

The Akita tightened his grip, clenching the chain about the detainee's neck the same way his own had been bound for so long.

Realizing he'd lost his only play for escape, the man deflated. He nodded in defeat as the Akita demanded he now free the retriever. This, however, would prove more logistically challenging, due to the length between the chains. There was no viable solution with the exception of releasing the chain from his neck if the man were to be able to reach the retriever.

Not to be deterred when they'd come this far, the dog made a snap decision. He dropped the chain from the man's neck and grasped his throat between massive canine jaws. He clung on gently, taking care to leave the man uninjured, yet held firmly enough that the threat was unmistakable.

The man began to thrash again now that both arms were free, but the Akita allowed his fangs to pierce his throat just enough to bring him back into line. He then dragged his captive by the neck closer to the retriever so that he was within reach of her collar.

Both dogs again pushed their demand into the man's mind. With the release of the Akita's chain, their control had slipped a notch; but he finally complied, reaching up and placing his thumb on the print reader. The retriever's chain dropped away.

This time, however, the accompanying beep was followed by a long, drawn-out alarm, causing ringing in their ears and immediate pain to both dogs.

So much for sneaking out of the compound to whatever fate awaited on the outside.

Panicked, the Akita quickly and without mercy took the life of the man, slashing his throat much as he'd done his partner. These men had caused unendurable suffering to the dogs for years; his policy in regards to them would not change simply because one had released them under duress. He would hold no remorse.

With the freedom from their chains and the dirty but necessary deed done, the intense fog over their brains lifted, and his mindlink with the retriever strengthened. Coordinating with each other through flashes of images and intuition, they took off toward the exit, feet pounding, hearts beating in stride.

They knew there was precious little time before backup arrived, and they had no intention of being around when it did.

He had no idea what the next turn would bring; but he now knew his name was Curjan, and he knew he had a job to do.

There was a girl out there, waiting.

Excerpt From
The Curse of Cur
The Chained Gods Series Book 2

by Tamira Thayne

I jumped out of bed, momentarily forgetting about my father slumbering in the chair next to me. My heart gave a tug at his presence, but this was no time for sentimentality. Unbidden, the words *I love you, Dad* whispered through my mind.

Fine, then, maybe just one second for schmaltz.

I couldn't afford to be side-tracked from my vision, I reminded myself—the vision that told me we needed to get to New York City, and fast.

Because I knew where the Akita we'd seen on screen yesterday, my father's second in command, was chained.

My mother is gonna flip her lid.

Mom hated cities in general, declaring them "the 2Ds"—dirty and dangerous—and to her, New York was not just any city, but THE city. THE TERRIFYING ONE.

I wasn't much of a fan, either...not that I'd ever been

there, so really, who was I to be all judgy-judgy. New York City always came off scary in the movies and TV shows, and between that and my mom's prejudice, I was onboard with any plans that boasted a NYC boycott.

Mom and I were similar in many ways, whether due to nature or nurture, I couldn't say. We were both country girls at heart, but we currently made our home in the small Virginia town of Culpeper, population 18,227, thank you very much. Our town flaunted a four screen movie theatre, a cutesy downtown shopping area complete with its own la-di-da French chocolate shop, and a host of local restaurants to choose from, including two recent additions of the Indian food variety. Yum.

The closest thing I'd seen to a gang in my town was the roving band of Pokemon Go players running amok and raiding virtual gyms on street corners, at landmarks, and in parks. I knew, because Mom and I had joined the Pokemon Go "gang" as our mother-daughter activity last year, hooking up with these marauders of mayhem and discovering the best places in town to catch the imaginary creatures.

I'd quickly gotten bored and moved along, but Mom could occasionally still be seen hanging with her PoGo friends, getting yelled at to "get a life" by irate shopkeepers, and bragging about the legendary "mons" she'd caught. Soon she was carrying her old phone and hotspotting into my account too, playing the game with what she termed her "virtual daughter."

She also claimed her virtual daughter was nicer than me. *Whatevs, Mom.*

Now that I thought about it, I was vastly underprepared to take on the streets of New York City.

As lovers of crisp country air and open skies, Mom and I still held tight to those dreams of a rural home, babbling on about the beauty and peacefulness of our fantasy retreat in the woods, our own kayakable river rambling along mere yards down the hill from our back deck.

There we would open our own animal sanctuary, where we'd spend all day loving on both our pets and the other critters we saved from certain death, while—in our imaginations at least—someone else did all the hard work of cleaning up and raising money. Yep, that was heaven.

Those dreams were far from my current reality.

Reality told me my father's (aka King Randulf's) top warrior was chained in dog form (don't ask) at a junkyard in New York City, and he needed us to come and yank him out of that mess. Ten to one he'd been left there to guard the second key to the destruction of two dimensions—Earth and Perrin—too.

Mwahaha. Yikes.

My father, who we'd released mere days ago from his own 18-year captivity as a chained German shepherd, was heartbroken over the conditions his warriors still endured. Knowing they were being tortured and starved for decisions he'd made was almost more than he could bear.

Now it was time for all of us to buck up. It was my mission, our collective mission, to find his chained warriors, unearth the remaining four keys, and rescue both Perrin and Earth from the grip of Phoebus, the scion, and their legion of minions.

Easy peasy.

I leaned heavily against the bathroom wall, toothbrush hanging out of my mouth.

Oh, who was I kidding.

The future looked daunting, indeed...

We hope you enjoyed Tamira Thayne's
*The Knight's Chain: A Chained Gods Series
Story, Vol 1.5* and this excerpt from *The Curse of Cur*.
This short story precedes *The Curse of Cur*,
and can be read before *Book 2*
or after to flesh out the character of the Knight.

**COULD YOU TAKE A MOMENT TO GIVE THE STORY
A SHORT REVIEW ON AMAZON.COM? YOUR REVIEWS
MEAN THE WORLD TO OUR AUTHORS, AND HELP THEM
EXPAND THEIR AUDIENCE AND THEIR VOICE.
THANK YOU SO MUCH!**

Find links to The Knight's Chain, The Wrath of Dog,
The Curse of Cur *and all our great books
on Amazon or at www.whochainsyou.com.*

Tamira Thayne pioneered the anti-tethering movement in America, forming and leading the nonprofit Dogs Deserve Better for 13 years.

During her time on the front lines of animal activism and rescue she took on plenty of bad guys (often failing miserably); her swan song culminated in the purchase and transformation of Michael Vick's dogfighting compound to a chained-dog rescue and rehabilitation center. She's spent 878 hours chained to a doghouse on behalf of the voiceless in front of state capitol buildings nationwide, and worked with her daughter to take on a school system's cat dissection program, garnering over 100,000 signatures against the practice.

She's the author of *The Knight's Chain, The King's Tether, The Wrath of Dog, The Cur of Cur, Foster Doggie Insanity, Smidgey Pidgey's Predicament, Spittin' Kitten's Speed-Away, Raffy Calfy's Rescue,* and *Capitol in Chains.* She's the editor of *More Rescue Smiles,* and the co-editor of *Unchain My Heart* and *Rescue Smiles.*

In 2016 she founded Who Chains You, publishing books by and for animal activists and rescuers.

Excerpt from

THE WRATH OF DOG: THE CHAINED DOGS SERIES BOOK 1

The hairy beast growled and lunged at me, his rusted logging chain straining to break—like it did every morning I cut down his back alley.

"I need to find another way to school," I grumbled to myself, heart pounding as I looked away and shuffled past him. No reason to deliberately provoke the Wrath of Dog, my oh-so-aptly-dubbed title for him.

Truth be told, I pitied the thing. "What kind of asshat chains their dog outside?" I furthered my inner rant.

At the age of 17 (and a half, thank you very much) I already had a heart for the animals, a trait pounded into my head by my bleeding heart mother from the time I could walk.

I could go on and on about dogs and chaining, Mom's monologue was just that stuck in my brain. "Dogs deserve better than life on a chain," she'd fume and fuss each time we passed a dog like Wrath.

Yeah, Mom, I get it. Someday I'll free Wrath and we'll rise up and smite his nasty-butt owner. For today, though, I just need to get past him without dying and make it the two blocks to class before the bell rings and I have another detention headed my way.

Sometimes it sucked to be me.

But never as much as it sucks to be Wrath, my do-gooder conscience—sounding suspiciously like my mother—reminded me.

Gah. Where was a dog biscuit when you needed one?

With one last glance to make sure the chain was holding, I took off at a run through the remnants of yesterday's skiff of snow and up to the doors of the high school.

Wrath's plight was soon forgotten.

"Bay!" the cheery scream echoed down the corridor. I cringed, my introvert soul longing to slink away unnoticed. But my Leo best friend would have none of that as long as she was still kickin', above ground, and had any air left in her lungs to bellow.

My exact opposite in every way, Amaya was short to my tall, loud to my quiet, and blond to my brunette.

She was curvaceous, cute, and sassy, whereas I was willowy and somber, with more of a girl-next-door thing going for me. Lucky me.

We shared a love of snark, all things fur-covered, and a devotion to each other that went beyond the high-school best friendships that were here one day, gone the next.

I did adore her.

But maybe not today. Today I wanted to turn and flee as all eyes in the crowded pre-first-period hallway swept my way....

Read more and order from whochainsyou.com, Amazon, and other outlets.

Also from Tamira Thayne

FOSTER DOGGIE INSANITY: TIPS AND TALES TO KEEP YOUR KOOL AS A DOGGIE FOSTER PARENT

Have you ever fostered a dog—happy to make a difference—but wondered why you felt frustrated and alone in your experience? Do you want to foster a dog, but don't know where to start, how to prepare, and what to expect? Have you experienced burnout or compassion fatigue in your rescue experience? If so, this is the book for you. Described as "an embrace from a friend who understands what we all go through; it is a beacon of hope to let other rescuers know they are not alone—a must-read for anyone involved in rescue."

This is not a book about dog training, but a book about people training while working with dogs...*Read more and order from whochainsyou.com, Amazon, and other outlets.*

www.ingramcontent.com/pod-product-compliance
Lightning Source LLC
Chambersburg PA
CBHW071230130626
46555CB00004B/1920